HORROR STORIES
TO TELL IN THE DARK

BOOK 1

SHORT SCARY HORROR STORIES
ANTHOLOGY FOR
TEENAGERS AND YOUNG ADULTS

BRYCE NEALHAM

HORROR STORIES TO TELL IN THE DARK: BOOK 1

Copyright © by Bryce Nealham.

All rights reserved. No part of this publication may be reproduced, distributed, or transmitted in any form or by any means, including photocopying, recording, or other electronic or mechanical methods, or by any information storage and retrieval system without the prior written permission of the publisher, except in the case of very brief quotations embodied in critical reviews and certain other noncommercial uses permitted by copyright law.

This is a work of fiction. Names, characters, business, events and incidents are the products of the author's imagination. Any resemblance to actual persons, living or dead, or actual events is purely coincidental.

CONTENTS

THE HOUSE ON MILLER ROAD 1
THE DESERT SHADOW 9
    Britney Supernault 17
LOCKED IN 19
    Frederick Trinidad 27
WITHIN THE LAKE 29
WHAT WE CAN'T SEE 41
    Maya Scianna 48
"MY DAD DID" 49
    Chase Wilkinson 56

Find Out About Our Latest Horror Book Releases...

Simply go to the URL below and you will be notified as soon as a new book has been launched.

bit.ly/3q34yte

"Quiet people have the loudest minds."

— Stephen King

HORROR STORIES TO TELL IN THE DARK: BOOK 1

THE HOUSE ON MILLER ROAD

By Britney Supernault

The house's squat, wood-planked exterior was even more depressing in person than in the photos.

Abandoned sometime in the '70s this house stood as an eyesore for everyone else living on Miller's Road.

According to the stories, I grew up hearing, as I was one of those people living on Miller's Road, three kids and one parent somehow got locked in the damp basement and died with eyes opened wide and mouths agape. Some squatters had discovered them, and their skin had begun to melt off their faces with maggots and flies devouring the rotting flesh.

The family of 4, all lined up the wall, staring placidly at the boiler room, with large chunks of their limbs missing after being feasted on by rats.

Now in my 30's with a wife and kid of my own, I had the hindsight to understand that those stories were made up. It would have made it into the news if they were true.

I looked the property up and down with contempt.

As one of the best real estate agents in my agency, I had been the obvious choice for when this dump came upon our desks. My boss cited me having grown up in the neighborhood as the second reason.

I looked down at my house file and back up at the ramshackle house, aged with various stains, graffiti, and dim, glass windows with a sigh.

I made my way to the steps. The wood was rotted away on the second step and the porch squawked with every timid step. I grabbed the keys from my pocket and quickly turned the lock, opening the door. I hoped to finish this inspection as quickly as possible.

The first thing that hit my senses was the dreary dark. Yellowed light from the grime-stained windows filtered through the living room, casting yellow squares on the floor.

Immediately after, my nostrils were assaulted by the smell of mildew and dust, which I could see fluttering through the dim light. I wiggled my nose as an inevitable sneeze racked my body.

I suddenly had the sense that someone was watching me.

I quickly wiped my nose and after haphazardly stuffing my pocket square into the pocket of my new suit, I did a quick survey of the room. Maybe a squatter had made his way in.

I did a quick sweep of the rest of the first floor, the floorboards bending underneath my weight as if they would give way any second.

All clear.

I would be surprised if there were any squatters. Even though the house had been empty for years, no druggies would go near it. They said that it gave off bad vibes.

Another eye roll, as I remembered looking down at the mismatched shoes, one with a large hole and a big toe sticking out of it, of the person who told me this outside the strip mall. I was 15 and I remember watching them roll their shopping cart away while whistling a tune.

Good riddance, it saved me a lot of work in the long run.

I went through the house with my checklist, making sure that key features were still intact.

"Just in case some poor sap wants to attempt to revamp the place." Smirked Kevin as he pushed the checklist into my hands earlier that morning. A couple of the other guys laughed, and I joined in when really, I wanted to-

Punch the guy?

"Hello?" I spun around in alarm, expecting to come face to face with a person, but all that was there were the hallway walls. It must have just been in my head. I mean they are my own thoughts. Of course, they're in my head, why would I have said that aloud.

But I could've sworn that I -

"Why stop there? Why stop there?"

I turned around again. Expecting somehow that someone had magically appeared in the last 10 seconds. But of course, I was the only person in the house.

I rubbed my ear with a sigh. Seems like the Tinnitus hadn't gone completely away yet.

I straightened up my suit before heading up the stairs taking two at a time. Once I got to the top of the stairs, I quickly made my rounds with the checklist.

3 bedrooms. Check.

Linen closet. Check.

Working hallway light. No. I flicked the switch up and down, but no light came on. As I scribbled down the notes, I heard the distinctive sounds of a screechy giggle that seemed to echo through the household. I peeked my head down the stairs, wondering if a kid wandered in, but no one answered. It must have been the neighbors.

I also wrote down 'family-friendly' in my notebook under 'selling features' for the property.

The last check was in the bathroom. The door was jammed shut, but with a few good hard shoves, I was able to wedge it open. I shimmied through the small gap and stood in the dingy bathroom.

All the fixtures were bad. And to top it off, in the middle of the room was a slight indentation into the floor with a drainage pipe.

Strange. I've never seen that in a house before.

I took a couple of steps closer and bent over to get a closer peek, wondering where it could possibly lead to when I saw two large eyes blink up at me.

I yelled and threw myself back against the wall. My breath came in heavy as my pulse pounded through my chest.

It was just googly eyes. It must have been. They seemed...almost human, but not quite. Too perfectly round. Too stark white in the dark, and the blue too bright. Some kid must have stuck their doll down there.

After slowing my heart rate down with a few meditative breaths, I began the slow climb over, back to the drainage pipe.

I peeked over the edge of the drain, which was no bigger than the size of my arm.

Nothing was there.

In confusion I dipped my head further down, peering into the drain as close as the cover would allow. I saw that it apparently opened into a wider space below, a space that wasn't marked on the house's blueprint.

I double-checked the papers again, just to make sure. Sure enough, it wasn't on there.

My thoughts were interrupted by the sound of feet moving. Scuffling against metal and echoing so it sounded like multiple pairs were moving. I peeked back down into the pipe, maybe rats had infested the house. It would align with the stori-

I saw that same pair of eyes; except now, they were farther back. Almost like I was staring at a pair of dimes in the distance. Their bright white color contrasted with the dark of the space. My heart began to thump in earnest as I reached for my cell phone light, flashing it down the drain.

The eyes stared back at me as it somehow moved about the space in a way I couldn't understand. They moved in and out of the light, shaped in an intricate pattern from the drain. They got closer. I couldn't stop staring at them. What did they belong to?

A rat? A fox? A cat?

The eyes then moved from the space further back, out of the light so I couldn't see them. I pushed my light farther in trying to see the eyes again.

Suddenly they appeared barely a foot in front of me, staring at me unblinking. I screamed and fell back from the drain.

I instantly knew I had to get out of there.

Mold. The house had mold and is making me see things. That must be it. At least that's what I told myself as I began to run. I heard the drain cap pop off as I attempted to squeeze out of the space between the jammed door and the wall. But I felt what I thought were large hands grab onto my leg.

I screamed as I was ripped from the doorframe and pulled back toward the drain. The claws ripped into the skin of my leg. I felt warmth run down my pant leg and I wasn't sure if it was piss or blood.

I grabbed onto the pipe underneath the sink, trying to hold on with all my strength. The thing was now trying to pull me into the drain.

I nearly passed out in pain and fear as my ankle bent into the drain. My arms gave way as nausea hit my stomach in waves. I was pulled to the center of the room.

My pants had ripped, and my skin was being taken off by the corrugated steel edges. My leg was being ground into the pipe like meat through a grinder. The pain was unbearable, and I let out another shriek as my knee dislocated as passed into the drain.

Tears and snot fell from my eyes, and I couldn't see.

I reached all around me until I grabbed a pipe that was run along the bottom edge of the wall. I pulled on it till it came loose and then I swatted the claws of the thing that had somehow melded into my own skin. I heard a giggle as the claws retracted.

I pulled my leg free and the sight of blood, and shredded flesh made me puke onto the floor. But the only thing on my mind was getting out of that damn house alive.

I tried to stand, and the pain was excruciating but I hobbled to the door. I squeezed into the hallway and tried to make it down the stairs, but my leg couldn't handle it and I tumbled down the stairs, slamming my head against the wall.

My vision was now blurry as I pulled myself towards the open entrance.

A small group of children stood, peeking through the fence and into the door. I yelled out to them reaching my hand out, hoping that one of them would have the good sense to get help, but their faces contorted in fear, and they all ran away, screaming in terror.

"No! No! Come back!" I yelled.

Come back. Come back. A voice imitated. It seemed to echo off the walls.

I screamed and crawled as fast as I could toward the door. Clawing the floor with my nails as I pulled myself forward.

Almost there. Almost there. I repeated in my head.

I heard the distinct sound of running in the walls beside my head. I felt tears of strain come pouring out. My leg was crushed, the blood pooling from it was leaving a streaked trail behind me.

Suddenly the front door slammed shut, the lock turned of its own volition.

I whimpered in agony as I helplessly crawled the last couple of feet, trying to reach up the door. But my hands couldn't turn the lock. I suddenly heard a door creak open. And quick steps emerge from what I instinctively knew was the basement. The steps almost waddled, rather than walked.

Weak, nearly passed out I turned and leaned against the door. I saw something pass quickly into the kitchen. The steps moved. And I heard the snicker. I felt around in my pockets for my keys. I desperately slid each key between each finger.

The thing stepped into the living room.

I felt my heart seize up and tears come to my eyes.

The thing was all white, a stark, pale white that looked almost sickly blue. It had two, no three, no four arms. Its skin was stretched taught over its body.

The most shocking feature was its face...or lack thereof. It was like sculptures in Greece, an almost human face but with what looked like a white stretched-out piece of silicone over it. The only facial features it did have was its round eyes. Stark white, blue in the middle, and staring straight at me.

I screamed as it came nearer to me. It seemed to stumble, using the four legs at once to walk in a waddling way.

"No. Please, God no. I have a child! A wife!"

"Oh, I know. You thought about them in the driveway. Oh, what a sweet, sweet family".

I whimpered as an arm stretched forward. Grabbing my non-hurt leg. It began to pull me. And I was too weak to do anything about it.

"Now with a father such as yourself... You'll make the perfect addition to my collection".

Its collection.

"Oh yes. My collection. A perfect family. Waiting for you downstairs. And no one will bother you down there. Human minds are so easy to manipulate".

I screamed and screamed as the thing pulled me towards the basement door, into that damp darkness down below where I knew would be sitting a family of four, a mother and her three children staring open-mouthed, eyes wide at the boiler room. The boiler room where this thing made its home.

Or perhaps this had been its home all along.

And I was now its decoration.

THE DESERT SHADOW

By Britney Supernault

I watched my parents pull out of the driveway on Halloween eve. I sighed. Babysitting duty. Again.

My parents had a conference thing at the last minute and so I was left with my little brother, Billy, who was now needing food to eat. As he kept repeating from the window left of me.

"Pizza! Pizza! I need some food or else my stomach will eat me!" His shrill 7-year-old voice chanted while watching our parents pull out of the long driveway.

"Dude, that's just hunger. Also, don't you have candy from school?" I said with a groan before turning around. I pulled the 100-dollar bill that my dad had handed me before leaving with strict rules: Order a pizza, tip the person, and then keep the rest for yourself.

Not bad for a weekend of babysitting. I demanded more than my usual rate due to it being Halloween and that we weren't going trick-or-treating this year.

"Yes. But I ate it all. Sugar is a wonderful thing." Billy said while still staring out the window. My parents were no longer in the driveway, and he was now staring at nothing but the darkness surrounding the forest.

"You are so weird," I said as I patted his hair with my hand. I left him staring out at nothing and went to order the pizza.

I couldn't blame him for being a bit off. He's seen way too many things, all within the last couple of months. And that's why I didn't mind spending some one-on-one time with him.

The first incident happened in the grocery store on our way back from Las Vegas.

On the way back, our car crapped out. We were stuck on the highway for hours. I had never been so bored.

Billy had to pee and after refusing to go with him, he went skipping, by himself to a large boulder in the desert. When he got back, he was crying and said that his shadow was too dark in the desert. I laughed at him, and he refused to talk to me, even when the car magically started, and we were back on the road.

We stopped at a grocery store in some seedy little town, grabbing snacks for the night since, due to the car crapping out and losing hours, we had to stay the night.

Billy walked to what I assumed was the toy aisle and I headed to the chip aisle. I don't remember if I heard the screaming first or if I felt the tug of Billy pulling on my sleeve first.

I followed him towards the screaming, I kept my hand clasped tightly around his wrist in case we needed to run. He turned down the aisle and to the back of the store, where the butcher was, and where a woman was hysterically crying.

I don't know what made me continue forward, I should've just turned back, but curiosity got the better of me. I saw the pool of blood first before I saw the man. He lay face up, his eyes empty, staring at the ceiling. Billy pointed at the man.

I couldn't take my eyes off the hysterical lady who was now on the ground. She just kept pointing at my brother and the body. She then began to grasp her chest and gasp for breath. She fell onto her face, splattering into the blood. Billy and I had smears of it on our faces and on Billy's hands. She died in front of us from fright.

My parents told us outside the grocery store, as the police made their rounds, that it was because she was old. Her death made more sense. The police questioned both my brother and me as we were one of the firsts on the scene and there weren't any surveillance cameras. Our parents didn't talk about the man with a knife in his chest.

The other incident was when Billy had gone to a sleepover with his friends, at the advice of his new psychiatrist, and came upon a dead body in the forest. He showed his friends the corpse.

A hiker had fallen off a short cliff and was impaled, face first, into a sharp branch of a tree. They said that his entire face had been swallowed by the branch. The blood ran down the tree and stained the dry grass a sick, deep, burgundy. The police marked it as an accidental death.

My parents quickly added Billy to a specialized child trauma psychiatrist's list of patients.

All things said, Billy was still the same. Quieter, and more conserved than other 7-year-olds, but still madly annoying and whiny.

Nonetheless, he was my little brother. That's why I wasn't too worried about babysitting. It meant pizza, movies, and candy. Everything any kid would find delight in.

Once all was said and done, bellies full of greasy pizza and $60 bucks in my pocket, it was time to tuck in for bed.

I carried Billy, who had passed out in the middle of the movie, upstairs to his bedroom which sat right across from mine. Once he was in bed, he had woken up and watched as I gently tucked his feet into his blue comforter.

"My shadow won't stop following me, Andy." Billy's voice was small with sleep. He rubbed his eyes as a large yawn took hold.

"That's what shadows are supposed to do buddy," I said with a roll of my eyes.

"But what about their bad words?" Billy asked as he rolled to face me, undoing my perfect tuck-in job.

"Shadows don't talk Billy." I looked at him with my brows furrowed. This kid really needed to go to bed.

"But he's so loud. And he said that he'd switch -" He suddenly shot straight up which caused me to yelp in surprise.

"What's the matter, dude? Gotta puke? You did heave down almost half the pizza." I said with a laugh as my heart rate slowed down from its racing pulse.

Billy's face contorted for only a moment; a moment so quick that I questioned if I had really seen it happen. Almost as if a shadow passed before his face.

Damn, I was probably the one who needed sleep.

Billy's face was now calm and serene. His sleepiness was gone, but he nonetheless laid down and pulled his sheets up to his chin.

"Shadows don't talk Andy." He said in a clear, small voice.

"No, Billy. They don't." I said hesitantly. What the hell just happened?

"I know they don't." He said matter-of-factly before turning over to face the wall.

"Oookay," I said as I patted his back and got up from his bed. He shivered in his blankets.

I quietly left the room, a puzzled expression on my face. I really don't understand Billy sometimes. But that's just being a kid. My mom told me all about my weird antics growing up – sometimes too much.

I went to the thermostat on the hallway wall and turned it up a degree or two before doing my house check and turning off the lights and locking the doors.

I flipped off the switch and took a deep breath before taking a slow stroll through the kitchen. I hated the dark, despite being in grade 9.

I'm fine. I'm fine. I'm fine.

But before I turned the corner, I heard what sounded like something tumbling down the stairs. I jumped out of my skin before reaching for the light. I scrambled to turn on the switch, rushing to check the staircase. Maybe Billy had sleep walked and fell.

But no one was around the staircase. And there was nothing that I could see that could have made the noise of tumbling down the stairs.

With a shiver, I realized that the door, opposite the staircase, leading to the basement, had somehow opened itself. I felt my stomach drop in fear and I raced upstairs as quietly as I could, scared that someone had somehow broken in.

I rushed into Billy's room, only to find his bed empty.

"Billy?!" I half-whispered, half-shouted into the dark of his room. I carefully checked his closet, opening it slowly and quietly whispering, "Billy?" as I looked.

Where had he gone?

As I turned from the closet, I heard the pitter-patter of scurrying feet across the rugged floor. I snapped around expecting to see my little brother standing behind me, but all I saw was darkness.

No, wait. This darkness, a shadow of sorts, was moving around from corner to corner.

In confusion, I watched the deep dark move from the corner in front of the bed to right in front of me. My heart hammered against my chest as I squinted into the sudden, deep darkness.

Suddenly two eyes opened - stark white with blue irises, in the darkness. I flinched in fear but was confused by the familiarity. They were like my little brother's eyes. I reached my hand out, but terror caused me to snatch my hand back and scream as a large, bright red mouth lit up with a sick, wide, pearl white smile.

In a panic, I grabbed a metal globe from the closet. I swung as hard as I could and heard the creature shriek and cry out with Billy's voice as it contacted the side of his face. I hit it again and again, intent on killing it right there and then. My hand became slippery with whatever blood this thing bled. I felt something cave in. It stopped screaming.

I almost didn't run but knew it was a trick; this monster had stolen Billy's voice. This was the shadow Billy was talking about.

I jumped the steps, four at a time, and ran straight into the basement, slamming the door behind me. I wiped my hands on my jeans and from the smear, on the white basement door, I saw that it was something colored like blood. I felt the pizza attempting to make a second appearance.

I basically fell into the basement, its stark empty cold contrast to the rest of our house. It smelt of mildew and wetness. I reached and pulled the cord for the light, more from memory than sight. I scanned the room, still scared that someone had broken in.

I flinched when my eyes landed on a single figure, crouched in the corner. My heart immediately softened when I recognized the dark hair, same as mine.

"Billy! Billy!" I yelled in relief as I ran to his figure.

He stood up as I wrapped my arms around him, enveloping him in a desperate hug.

"We have to go buddy, something, the shadow, it's upstairs. We need to go, I believe you. Let's go. NOW!" I said into his hair as I kissed the top of his head.

"I know what's upstairs." Billy said in a monotone voice. Except it wasn't his voice. This one was shriller but somehow smooth. I pulled back to check on my little brother.

What I saw made my blood freeze, my heart stop, and every hair stand up on end.

I saw something like my brother. Except the smile was much too wide and too bright red. Its eyes were white surrounding black, and I could see cracks in his skin as if he were broken pottery.

I screamed and fell to my knees.

Now face to face with whatever the hell had stolen my brother.

"Andy?" The sickly shrill voice spoke, its neck twisted almost horizontal as his head kept twitching.

"You're not my brother." That was all I could choke out.

"Oh, no? Well, I'm the only one you've got. You see, you already dealt with your other brother." His hand pointed to my own, still slick with blood, what I now understood was blood.

I felt tears stream from my eyes as realization hit, nausea crashed over me in waves, and I was sick on the basement floor. I felt my head go dizzy and flipped onto my back as stars filled my vision. The soulless eyes and blood-red mouth stood over me.

"But I'm afraid that I can't be your brother anymore. His body is much too old now. Once my shadow, or your brother, in this case, is gone then this body starts falling apart at the seams. It happens every time. And then I get stuck in places like the desert" The thing tsked, "Nasty place, the desert."

I whimpered as the face drew closer to mine.

"I guess you will have to do."

ABOUT THE AUTHOR

Britney Supernault

Britney Supernault, also known as the Cree Nomad, hails from the wintery north of Alberta, Canada. Coming from the small community of East Prairie Metis Settlement, Britney is proud of her Métis Cree background and settlement but is most often seen out of country.

An avid traveler, Cree Nomad is an experienced freelance writer, specializing in travel articles, but hopes to expand into the world of fiction by becoming an author herself. She hopes to publish her first novel in the next two years.

Having written and delivered over 120 articles this year alone, Britney prides herself as being 'the most determined writer you will ever meet'. Working mainly through the freelancing platforms Fiverr and Upwork, you can find the Cree Nomad seated at a café in some faraway country with a coffee in hand and her eyes trained on her laptop.

You can read more of her work in her personal blog at Creenomad.com, or by visiting her Instagram page: Cree_Nomad.

If you'd like to hire her for any articles, blog posts, or your ghostwriting needs, feel free to contact her through her Fiverr or Upwork profiles, or email her at: thecreenomad@gmail.com.

LOCKED IN

By Frederick Trinidad

A loud ringing sound inside my head woke me up from a restless sleep. I opened my eyes but I saw nothing but pitch-black darkness. "What the hell is going on?" I asked myself.

My pupils dilate in order to conceive what little light the room has to offer. As I opened my eyes wider, I could only make out what seemed to be the ceiling of a room.

I could not move at all but I was able to smell the faint scent of chemicals all around me.

"Where the hell am I?" was the next question I asked myself.

The answer to that question came in the form of a sudden burst of light, temporarily blinding my eyes. My eyes hurt so much but for some reason, I couldn't close them.

The blinding light continued to invade my eyes until they gradually adjusted and corrected my vision. Two men dressed in white overalls came into my view. They quietly looked down at me, both standing from my right side.

I wanted to speak but words refused to escape my mouth. The two men left my view and I heard them exit as the door banged on their way out.

Panic started to take over me as I assessed my situation. My peripheral visions could make out a white sheet to my left and a tiled wall to my right. The tiles were the kind you could see in most bathroom walls.

I wanted to see what that white sheet was but I could not move my head to the side. Heck, I couldn't even move my eyeballs to have a better look at it.

I heard the door open and one of the men in white came into my view again. This time, he wrote notes on a clipboard as he simultaneously looked at my face.

Fear struck me as he reached out his hand to touch the right side of my face but felt relief as he gently moved my head to the left in order to inspect the backside of my head.

With this move, my head was now facing my left side and plainly saw what I have been toiling to see. The white sheet was fully covering the body of a person. The rest of my view made out what seemed to be silhouettes of other dead bodies lying across the room.

A horrific feeling of terror swept over me as I came to the realization: "I am in a morgue and I lay as one of the cadavers".

My heart pounded to the point of hurting my chest and I could loudly hear every beat as though it was counting down my extinction.

The man in white moved my head to its original position, making me face the ceiling again. And as he moved his face closer to mine, I started screaming at him but not the faintest of sounds were produced by my mouth.

"Hey, I'm still alive!" I tried screaming at him. But he just looked at me not noticing anything beyond what he expected.

I tried grimacing at him, hoping he would notice the change in my expression. But sadly, there was no reaction from him nor was I able to produce any movement to my facial muscles.

In a desperate effort to escape my horrible predicament, I tried moving my limbs.

First, I focused on moving one of my toes, when that didn't work, I tried moving my fingers but it didn't work either. And to my grim realization, I couldn't even blink.

The man then moved across the room to pick up a device of some sort. As he walked closer back to me, I began to see what it was. It's a damn toe tag.

"Oh hell no!" I thought to myself in anticipation of how much his action would hurt me.

I held my breath in the horror of what is to come. I'd close my eyes if only I could. And then the man used it to clip one of my toes.

A horrible, shooting pain resonated from the spot but it's as if my entire body felt it and I wanted to yell in so much pain.

Unable to let out a scream, I began to feel dizzy and felt like I would faint. But I didn't lose consciousness, in fact for whatever reason, I was still very much alert.

The other man came in and to my horror, he said the other guy tagged the wrong toe and the error needs to be rectified. You may very well conclude what happened next.

Some time passed by, and save for the cadavers in the room, I was left alone. Both my toes were tagged and I've grown accustomed to the pain emanating from my lower limbs.

I can't remember how it happened but my head was slightly tilted to my left, giving me a full view of the corpse laying on the bed next to mine.

Then my mind seemed to start playing tricks on me because I could swear, I noticed movements from the body.

I brushed off the thought, wondering when will those two men go back so I could continue trying to make them realize I wasn't dead like they thought.

But then the body moved again.

This time, it wasn't just the slight movement that I noticed earlier. "What the hell?!" I remarked in freezing horror.

The next thing it did was slowly but deliberately get up to a seated position and start getting off the bed. The sheet still covered its entire body save for both its pale arms sticking out from the sides.

And then, it turned and started hovering towards me.

The only thing I could do is watch as the ghastly figure slowly placed its cold, lifeless palm upon my mouth and gripped it tightly, almost suffocating me.

And then, quickly and sickeningly, it turned my head to the right, revealing the heart rate monitor connected to me.

It is flat-lined.

I gasped for air as I violently woke up from the horrible nightmare. I strained my eyes to see that the corpse to my left was still lying as it always did.

To my relief, it was just a dream. However, my whole predicament was still the same. I was still in that dreaded room in a dreaded locked-in syndrome.

The two men in white overalls weren't there and every corpse was still in their proper places. And then I thought of being back home.

I miss playing video games, watching shows on the internet, and enjoying all sorts of home entertainment while living off my parents' income.

All my brothers and sisters have left home and are living on their own. From my teenage years, I've chosen to hide away from the world while avoiding social contact.

Through that life of isolated living, I came to learn the deeper workings of the internet. I could not describe the feeling of joy and excitement I started to have the moment I discovered the far reaches of the World Wide Web.

But then, my daydreaming was disrupted by a loud bang from the door and I was back to that horrendous reality. The men in white entered the room carrying what looked like a canister connected to some sort of device.

To my horror, I realized it was the siphoning device used for the embalming process. I couldn't remember how I knew what it was.

One of them walked towards a table stand on the wall, placed the canister atop of it, and then pulled the stand right beside me.

Despite being an atheist, I prayed like I never prayed before, desperate for salvation. Then I thought, this whole scenario was just too unreal to be true.

"I'm still asleep and this is just a dream. Wake up damn it! Wake up!" I scolded myself.

But all hope was purged off of me the moment I realized things weren't happening as I wanted them to. I wasn't waking up from a horrid nightmare.

All of it was a reality. I then decided to succumb to the inevitable hoping it would just be over soon.

Then one of the men gave a long, curious look at my eyes. "Hey, his pupils are dilating." He called out to the other man.

A great sense of hope and relief took over my emotions. I was going to be saved and in my mind, I kept thanking the man for noticing my actual state.

The other man hurriedly came over and inspected my eyes as well.

"Hey don't worry, we'll take care of you. Just sit tight and we'll be right back" He assured me then he and the other man exited the room once again.

They must've been gone for several minutes when my feelings of great relief quickly turned into feelings of new misery.

"Am I going to live for the rest of my life in this sorry state?" I miserably thought to myself.

As my mind processed the new scenario, the same man who assured me earlier entered the room again. He then moved to my side and talked to the wall over my head.

"He's been tearing up the whole time." He announced.

Then I curiously thought; "Who is he talking to? What the hell does he mean I was tearing up the whole time?"

I agonizingly used my entire vision to investigate everything that I could see. Then right from the upper corner of my eyes, I made out what looked like the lens of a camera pointing directly down at me.

Towards the right, I saw a portion of the heartbeat monitor displaying a normal heart rate. I must've seen it before but never cared to notice it.

"Why is there a camera pointed at me? And, if they thought I was dead, then why the hell do they need to connect me to a heart rate monitor?" I questioningly surveyed my situation.

And then, my heart dropped to the full extent of my reality.

"They knew I was alive the whole time." I horrifyingly concluded.

Fear and exasperation began to set in as I discovered the kind of people I was dealing with. I then knew who they were and what they were doing.

These are the kind of people who bears no remorse and take pleasure in giving pain to their hapless victims. They happily provide contents that feed the perverse hunger of their online audiences.

And I now lay as their latest offering.

"Today, we present to you, the embalming of a man who we paralyzed. And like in every one of our experiments, no anesthetic of any kind is to be administered." The man declared as he disgustingly smirked at the camera.

My mind began racing to understand how it all came about. The last thing I remember was falling asleep on the bed in my room. Then I realized that they must have tracked me down using the I.P. address of my computer.

And now, there I was, existing on the other side of the spectrum.

I often watched those videos while eating popcorn as men and women get tortured to death. I've seen a video of these men in white overalls using the siphoning device to suck the blood out of a living woman, and that's how I knew what the device is.

Being an avid viewer of their dark web snuff videos, they must've decided it was my turn to be in one of their contents. Amid my scenario, my mind began playing the cartoon of a light bulb turning on and Tweety bird telling me that I'm now the star of the show.

"Hey yeah! It's my turn to shine." I told myself with strange but fulfilling satisfaction.

At the same time, an old, 70's psychedelic music started playing in my head. I thought for a moment that I was going insane because I was very amused by it all.

"We won't paralyze the next one and compare the ratio of their heartbeats."

The man in white overalls said as he finally approached me and plunged the sharp, siphoning device deep into my lower abdomen. Like a famished beast, the device gluttonously sucked my blood and slowly drained the life off of my body.

All the fun and amusement went away as fast as they came.

I felt no sense of glamour and no sense of pride which I expected given that I was the star of the show.

All I felt was pain, horrible, gruesome pain as my body thread towards a slow, painful death.

But it's all justified I suppose,

As Peter Kürten once said; "That would be the pleasure to end all pleasures."

ABOUT THE AUTHOR
Frederick Trinidad

Frederick has been in the business of ghostwriting for a couple of years now. He wrote blogs for brands, web articles, social media posts, and scripts for different YouTube channels.

However, writing stories has been his passion since childhood and this anthology is his way of expanding his writing career and reaching a wide range of audiences.

He discovered his love for horror storytelling during the peak of the pandemic when the world held its breath amidst a global state of uncertainty. His innovative style of writing is designed to make readers experience his distinctive brand of horror and mystery for themselves.

Fred wrote a mystery/thriller novel that he works to see published by the first quarter of 2022. The short story contributions that he imparted in this anthology shall give you a peek at the horror that awaits you in that book and his literary works in the future.

To receive updates from his work, you can follow his personal Facebook account at: https://www.facebook.com/frederick.trinidad.3

You can also reach him via email at: trinidadfred79@gmail.com

WITHIN THE LAKE

By Maya Scianna

My friend Sammy stood on a rock holding his girlfriend, Jenny's bikini top while she covered herself and squealed at him, "Give it back you shit!" She was probably going to dump him later.

"Come and get it!" Sammy called out to Jenny who was standing in the sand shivering and topless. I watched as he cannonballed into the lake from the small cliffside.

He swam over to me, where the water was only up to his shoulders. My feet barely touched the sand and I could feel the slimy algae between my toes. "This is why your relationships don't last long," I told him.

He shrugged his shoulders and splashed me with water. I splashed him back and ripped the bathing suit out of his hands, "Hey!" I started swimming away as fast as I could.

"Catch!" I called out and threw the bathing suit as far as I could as I was instantly pulled underwater. I closed my eyes and tried to come up for air, but he wasn't letting go. *What the hell!*

I tried to tug my leg harder and wouldn't budge, so I kicked him and my foot met his face. He immediately let go and I swam to the surface. I came up gasping for air and choking. They were both staring at me, and Sammy had already swum back to shore, "What?"

"You forget how to swim?" Sammy asked as he shook his hair and dried himself off with a beach towel.

"What? You're the one who pulled me down," Sammy raised his eyebrows and gave me a side-eye. "Anyway, how did you get over there so fast?" I said, treading through the shallow water and wringing out my tangled brown hair.

"What are you talking about?"

"You grabbed my leg and pulled me under!"

"I didn't."

"What- I," I turned and looked at the murky water that moved in tiny waves carrying away debris and colored leaves.

"He was debating coming after you when he realized you weren't just being dramatic," Jenny said coming out from behind a tree tying her bikini top around her neck. Her brows furrowed and her eyes filled with concern.

"Let's go back to the cabin and eat dinner," Sammy said. I was staring at the lake, looking for something. Anything.

All that I saw was the sunset's reflection bouncing off the water making the water appear pink and orange. Suddenly I heard the crunching of leaves and felt a warm hand grab my arm, making me jump. Immediately the hand let go.

"Sorry." Jenny said, "You just looked a little pale."

"It's fine." I turned and followed Sammy who was already up the rocky hill sitting on the rock on the cliffside.

We walked back to the cabin that Sammy's parents had let him use for the weekend. He wanted it to just be him and his girlfriend, but his mom refused to leave them there alone and told him to bring a friend.

I couldn't turn down getting away from my parents and being in a warm and cozy cabin in the woods. I'm somehow the responsible friend, not sure how I ever earned that title.

Maybe it was the good grades. It sure wasn't the sneaking out all the time and getting drunk on playgrounds and in parking lots with groups of other teenagers.

The cabin sat in the middle of the forest about two miles away from the winding road that led back to civilization. Moss spread on the stone along the bottom exterior of the house. The dark wooden logs climbed up to the roof where a stone chimney peaked over the green stained wooden roof that was beginning to fade in some places.

A fire pit sat a few feet from the wooden staircase, a fire hazard within another fire hazard. Strong winds could send flames that would easily swallow the flammable building.

My stomach grumbled, "Hotdogs tonight??" I asked.

"Sure, I'll start the fire," Sammy said.

"I'll get the buns and hotdogs out of the cooler."

"I'll follow Zoe," Jenny said and followed me up the wooden steps into the cabin. When we were behind closed doors, she asked, "Are you okay? It really did look like someone dragged you under. Sammy wasn't paying attention so he didn't see it, but I did."

"Honestly, I don't know." Chills ran down my arms and I crossed them over my chest.

"Let me know if you need anything," Jenny said and removed hotdog buns from the wooden cabinet. I pulled out the twenty-something hot dogs that Sammy had forced into a zip lock bag that couldn't be closed all the way. His solution was to put that zip lock bag into a plastic grocery bag without actually tying the bag closed.

"Boys," I muttered and rolled my eyes.

Jenny threw her head back and laughed, "Sounds about right," She was beaming

We headed back outside and found Sammy sitting on a camping chair, smoking a cigarette next to the fire. "Where the hell did you even find those?" I asked.

"They were inside my dad's jacket that I borrowed from him. Doubt mom knows about it." He replied casually.

The sun was already setting behind the mountains. Glowing light cast shadows on Sammy's face, making his facial features stand out. He tossed the cigarette into the pit, the fire crackled.

After we'd eaten, Sammy had pulled out a six-pack of bud-light and tossed one to me, who fumbled and almost dropped it. "Nice catch," Sammy snickered.

"Asshat, and seriously, bud light?"

"Beggars can't be choosers."

A rustling sound caught my attention from the trees, bushes shuffled and twigs snapped. "What is that?"

"Probably a raccoon or something." Sammy replied, "You're just paranoid from earlier, you're fine." He took a sip from the beer. "My family has been coming here since before I was born."

"Didn't your sister die here?" I asked and immediately regretted it; the beer had worn my filter down. "I'm sorry, I shouldn't have said that."

Sammy became tense. We all sat in silence for a few minutes before he finally said, "She drowned in the lake, still don't know how or why."

"Why do you guys still come here?" Jenny asked, then hesitated and said, "I'm sorry, you don't have to respond if you don't want to."

He shook his head, "We do it because it's almost like we still get to visit her."

I looked away towards the forest and a pair of glowing eyes met mine. Every part of my body froze, I was sure my heartbeat had stopped for a couple of seconds.

The empty, white eyes held me there in a trance, I couldn't find the strength to look away.

"Zoe!" Sammy exclaimed. I jumped.

"What?"

"You were practically in a trance, you wouldn't respond," Jenny replied, staring in the direction I just was.

"I'm sorry," I replied

Sammy's voice lowered, "Are you okay?"

"I think so." I tugged my jacket sleeves over my hands and hugged myself.

"I think we should go back inside," Jenny said, moving rather quickly, "I feel a bit uneasy."

"Are you sure?" Sammy asked and Jenny nodded. "Fine, maybe things will be better tomorrow." He looked a little irritated, but he chose not to say anything else. He left the fire going.

"Shouldn't we put that out?" Jenny asked.

"Nah, we're fine."

I glanced back to where I'd seen the eyes, but all that looked back was absolute darkness. "Come on, let's go," Jenny called to me, holding her pink and white quilt around her shoulders. Her borderline platinum hair sat on her head in a messy bun with tiny hairs attempting to escape.

I went to bed early and I made sure that the window was locked. I'd wished there were curtains that I could close. I put out the light on my lantern and crawled under the soft knit blanket Sammy's mom let me borrow.

"It gets super cold up there, that thin blanket that you're trying to bring won't do anything." She'd said, and she was right. I had layered both my blanket at hers, but I was still shivering. I eventually started to doze off.

Tap. Tap. I came back to reality for a second, but my eyes were heavy and I gave in to sleep again.

Tap. Tap. Tap. It was louder this time. I sat up, wrapped my blanket over my shoulders, and rubbed my eyes. *Tap. Tap. Tap. Tap.*

"What the-" I looked at the window and found someone looking back. *Tap. Tap. Tap.* It continued. There was someone out there. She had long hair that fell into uneven pieces around her eyes with the rest tanged into knots.

Her eyes were white slits that were swollen along with the rest of her face. Water dripped from her hair and down her pale blue face.

I was paralyzed with fear when the latch on the window came off from the inside and she used her bony fingers that were swollen at her fingertips, to slide the window open.

She let out a low gurgle and water poured from it. She crawled through the slightly ajar window and I took that opportunity to make a run for it, but the knob wouldn't budge, "Help!" I cried out in desperation and pounded on the door.

I started kicking and slamming my body into it until I felt ice-cold slimy hands around my mouth and neck. My screams were muffled but I kicked and fought for my life. Then she quickly turned and thrust me face-first into the door and I slumped to the ground.

"Zoe?" I heard from behind the door, but the room was spinning and the voice didn't sound familiar. I touched my forehead and felt something wet drip from my forehead and onto the palm of my hand; I let out a pitiful cry.

The thing forced its face in mine and grinned with crooked, bloody teeth and swollen lips. I felt its rank, cold breath hit my face.

It continued to make a gurgling noise and a sound that I could only describe the sound as similar to the grudge movie I'd watched at nine years old when I wasn't supposed to. Water trickled down from its tangled hair and landed on my leg. I tried to scream again, but it forced its fist down my throat and licked the blood dripping from my head with its slimy and rubbery tongue.

Hot tears escaped my eyes and I weakly tried to grab the thing's arm and remove its hand from my throat. To my surprise, it let me and retreated towards the window. It lifted a finger to its lips. It then contorted its body into a position that reminded me of a spider. *Pop. Pop. Pop. Pop.*

Its head turned 180 degrees and faced me as it moved like a spider and crawled back through the window and into the night. I turned and heaved until the hotdogs I'd eaten earlier were on the floor. I wasn't ever eating hotdogs again.

The door flew open and Sammy and Jenny raced into the room, their eyes practically bulging from their eye sockets. Their faces faded away from me and the world went white.

That was the last time that I had full control over my own body for a while. The next time I opened my eyes and I was just watching myself, it was like a dream. It was my body moving, but it wasn't me.

"Why did you try to drown yourself in the lake?" The shell of me stayed silent.

The doctor sighed, "We won't make any progress if you keep this up. Don't you want to see your family again?"

Yes. I said from the part of my brain that I was locked inside of. It was like, well, being in a psych ward like this. I could have kicked and screamed and called for help, but I'd lost complete control over my life.

The doctor handed me pills and told me to take them, "These will make you feel better, give them a try." Next, he offered me a cup of water. "I'm going to stay here until you take the pills." I begrudgingly swallowed the pills. "Good. I'll send in a nurse to bring you something to eat." He left us alone.

I paced around the room and trailed my fingers along the cold cemented walls and along the cracks and indented lines before placing my whole hand against it. Tiny grains of dust stuck to the palm of my head.

I inhaled and closed my eyes. The room smelled like plastic and rubbing alcohol and I felt the cold tile flooring through the socks the hospital provided me with. Then I sat on the bed and felt the rough texture of the sewing lines on the thin white blanket.

Then, something stirred in my stomach that reminded me of the waves of the ocean. I raced to the bathroom and murky green water poured out of my mouth like a faucet and into the toilet. I felt the barrier between me and my mind loosen and I was able to get back into the driver's seat for a brief moment before I was overpowered and forced back in.

My shell flushed the toilet, gripped the sink, and spat out excess revolting water that had a metallic taste down the drain. I stumbled out into the bedroom area and looked up into the safety mirror in the corner of the room. Only, it wasn't me looking back, the face wasn't mine. "Stop it!" It growled.

The door opened, "Your friends are here to see you." She said, "Also, I brought you a sandwich."

Without even checking the contents, I practically inhaled the thing and felt a lump drop into my stomach. The nurse didn't seem concerned, "The doctor changed his mind about letting anyone see you. We hope that seeing your friends will make you feel a little better, and your mom and dad are on their way up here".

Again, I didn't speak, but she led me out of the room and another nurse joined on the other side of me as we walked. They led me down the hall, passing other rooms that were like mine. I heard a woman sobbing loudly from behind the door at the end of the hall and a man screaming from behind another.

They took me into a room at the end of the hall that had a wooden table, chairs, and a locked cabinet. Two of those chairs were taken by Sammy and Jenny.

I felt warmth spread through me at the sight of them. I started fighting the barrier again to get to them, putting all of my might into it. The nurses told us they would be in the hallway and will be keeping an eye on us, and then they were gone.

"Zoe." That was all Sammy said. His eyes held dark circles and his hair was a disheveled mess of golden blonde hair. He looked like he hadn't slept in a week. Jenny didn't look too great either.

Her hair was still in a messy bun but it was loose and falling to the side.

She wasn't wearing makeup, but remnants of mascara stayed behind and emphasized the black and puffy dark circles under your eyes.

I smiled and their faces dropped, "Hello, brother." Again, not my voice.

"What?" Sammy replied, his voice shaky and higher than normal.

"You know me," I said again, then lunged over the table and grabbed him by the neck. I kept pushing, trying to make myself stop.

I begged her *Please stop, let him go! He doesn't deserve this!*

"Oh, but he does." Jenny was screaming for help, but the nurses weren't able to enter the room. The door was being held shut by a force I couldn't describe.

It was like anger radiated off of my body and took over the energy in the room, gaining control of everything in this room. Jenny tried to push me off of Sammy who was gasping for breath with his eyes starting to roll to the back of his head.

No! I shoved her away and let go of Sammy and watched his lifeless body fall to the floor, hitting his head on the corner of the table on the way down.

I turned and puked out more lake water until it turned black with the consistency of molasses. She was gone, and Sammy was dead. I collapsed onto the floor and found Jenny shaking Sammy's corpse. The nurses rushed in and grabbed me by the arms. I thrashed and screamed at the top of my lungs.

More people rushed in and pulled me away. "Sammy" I screamed.

I watched what looked like a projection of Sammy, watching Jenny, his face full of sorrow. The girl from the lake was hugging him, the sides of her mouth pulled into a smile she looked at me.

"Thank you."

WHAT WE CAN'T SEE

By Maya Scianna

"You need to let us know when you need to use the restroom," the nurse said with her arms crossed against her chest. Her short, blonde hair curved in and hugged her round cheeks. She was getting frustrated with Charlotte.

"And let you guys watch me pee? No thanks." Charlotte said, dragging her rattling IV pole and pulling herself back onto the hospital bed. Her arms were shaking.

The nurse shook her head, her lips pulled into a straight line. She didn't want to watch Charlotte pee either, but it was her job. "Please let us know next time, we need to monitor your urine and check it for ketones." She was happy to leave soon so that someone else could deal with Charlotte.

Charlotte didn't respond. She knew she was being standoffish, but she wasn't coping well with her new diagnosis. She was angry, and in some ways, she was taking it out on them.

She thought back to when she hadn't known what was wrong with her, and she could have gone about her day without thinking about it. They say ignorance is bliss, but it's only partially true.

One wrong decision in a situation in which you know nothing could lead to the worst possible outcome.

"I'll be leaving for the afternoon. Your night nurse is going to be Anne," the nurse said as she erased her name, Cece. Cece took one last look at Charlotte, adjusted her IV, then left the room, but left the door ajar.

Charlotte hadn't intended to fall asleep, but the lack of sleep made her fall asleep in a hospital bed that felt like a flat stone. The rattling of the metal cart that was periodically brought into the room to draw blood is what startled her awake.

She kept the blanket over her head, putting off the prick of another needle and then being told she needed to order food off of the limited hospital menu that was specifically for diabetes. Only, the menu was more catered to people with type two, not type one.

The choices of food were completely bland. Charlotte craved a whole meal, not a tiny ham sandwich without any condiments and unseasoned mashed potatoes. She didn't know how they managed to make them taste so bad, especially when packet mashed potatoes tasted better than that.

Charlotte groaned and finally pulled the covers off, but there was nobody there, only a metal cart beside the bed. Her eyebrows furrowed and she wrapped her fingers around the metal IV pole and slid out of the bed, letting her feet fall onto the cold hospital floor.

Charlotte had refused to wear the socks they offered her because they reminded her of her grandma when she'd died in this very hospital. The nurses just assumed that she was being a stubborn teenager.

The door to the room was wide open, so Charlotte assumed that someone had entered the room and left before she was fully awake. She ran her fingers along the stainless steel surface and peeked under it, but there was nothing to see. "I hate hospitals." She said, pushing the cart out of her way.

Charlotte turned towards the empty doorway and peered into the empty hallway. She wondered where everybody was and why it couldn't be this silent late at night when she was trying to sleep. She stepped out onto the grey carpet and followed the black designs on the gray carpet down the hallway, carefully pulling the IV pole with her, wishing she could just remove the needles in her arm. It was so silent that she could hear every step she took, making her feel uneasy.

Ding. Charlotte's head took a sharp turn towards the elevators she was passing. Her dark, golden-brown hair swayed past her with her sudden halt, and she made eye contact with a man pulling a long metal cart with a sheet covering what Charlotte could only assume was a human body based on the shape.

"Wait-." she called, but the doors closed. Charlotte stumbled towards the elevator almost pushing over the IV pole and pushed the button. It immediately opened.

"What the hell?" She stuck her head inside first before getting in.

Confused, Charlotte pressed the button for the first floor. *I could use a snack*, she thought about the mini cafe by the lobby. Only the button wasn't lighting up, something was broken. Charlotte tried to step out of the elevator, but it quickly shut before she could. She even stuck her arm out to set off the sensors, but the elevator was ready to take her arm off.

The elevator began rapidly descending, reminding Charlotte of the Tower of Terror ride at Disneyland. She grabbed hold of the metal bars with one of her hands and almost collapsed. Her IV bag swung back and forth on the metal hook almost falling off.

Then it stopped and opened its doors to another white hallway, the end of the metal cart she'd seen the man in the elevator with, was sitting at the end of the hallway. The stranger was nowhere to be seen. The wall covered the bottom half of the body on the cart.

The torso, and above were all that Charlotte could see. The lights flickered, and a chill breeze made Charlotte shiver. The head turned and faced her and she froze. Charlotte felt her pulse quicken, she wanted to run but didn't know where. She debated ripping out the needles but she didn't know how to remove them without hurting herself. She

The cart rolled down the hall until it was no longer in Charlotte's sight as if someone was pulling it away. Charlotte let go of the breath she was holding and rapidly hit the elevator buttons. The doors held themselves open, and the buttons didn't light up. She was stuck.

"Come on, come on, please." Charlotte fought the urge to cry, panic crawled up her chest, making it difficult for her to breathe. She shook her head, "No, no no no come on!"

The elevator refused to cooperate. She knew the only way she could go was towards where she'd seen the body. She needed to get out, and if she had to drag the IV pole up the stairs, she would try.

The hallway split into two different directions, Charlotte thought she was safe choosing to go left, away from the body she saw. She walked, eyes peeled and on high alert. When she passed the area where she saw the body, she kept her eyes locked in the opposite direction where she was walking. She didn't know that she was being watched by the world of the dead.

She jumped when she passed her reflection in a decorative mirror on the white wall. Her face was pale, her eyes were dark, and her cheeks were sunken in. Charlotte reached up and touched her dark and tangled hair, it felt rough and frizzy.

Her frame was thin, her skin was stretched over her bones, the shape of them defined by her tight skin. She was decomposing in front of her eyes. Charlotte watched as her skin dripped off of her face like wax on a candle and gripped her face to check if it was still attached to her bones, feeling relieved when she felt it still intact.

Charlotte covered her face and rubbed her eyes before looking back up again, and started screaming. The man she'd seen in the elevator was standing right behind her in the mirror.

Then he wrapped his hands around her neck and pushed her up the wall, holding her there, letting her feet dangle and kick. The needles ripped out of her arm and the IV pole fell to the ground, the sound of metal hitting the tile. Her weak, shaky hands reached up in an attempt to remove the cold, rubbery ones from around her neck.

The man looked at her with a slimy smile and malicious eyes. Charlotte noticed that his features were similar to hers, his thin and frail body matching hers. When her vision started to fade to white, he let go. He wasn't finished toying with her yet.

Then he faded away and Charlotte fell to the ground landing on her ankle at an odd angle. She let out a sharp wheeze and choked, gently holding her neck where the man's hands had been. Round red marks were left behind the reminder of this encounter.

Charlotte let out a raspy breath, tears slipping from her eyes. She didn't understand what was happening to her. Blood dripped from her forearm and onto her green hospital gown. She looked pitiful, different from the facade she'd had put on earlier.

Charlotte could barely see through spots dancing in her vision. She was suddenly picked up and strapped down to a metal table. She was then being pushed down a long hallway to a big room. Everything was blurry and bright.

Her eyes struggled to adjust, so she just shut them. She found herself just wanting the experience to end and to die. Nobody would miss her anyway.

Charlotte laid in a room by herself strapped to a table, surrounded by square metal doors stacked on each other in a wall like the lockers at her school gym. She could feel a slight breeze on her forearm, reminding her of the blood that was continuously dripping down. Metal cases began to rattle and shake vigorously. She felt hot tears pooling in her eyes.

Out of Charlotte's peripheral, she noticed one of the boxes open like a drawer, bony feet coming out with it. She felt her body stiffen and all she could do was stare and listen to the crackling of worn bones. It left her vision and floated away, but still hung around nearby.

Silence filled the room again, and Charlotte hoped it had left her alone. Unbeknownst to her, it stood behind her with hungry eyes, it had been a while since he'd been able to tamper with something alive.

Her heartbeat echoed in her ears, and the corpse heard it too. She moved her wrists to find out how strong the straps were, but they wouldn't even budge. She tried moving around in different directions, but the cloth was starting to rub off her first layer of skin.

Charlotte stopped and looked at her surroundings. To her left, she could see a scalpel on a metal tray nearby, on top of a cart. Different tools that Charlotte didn't recognize were also spread evenly across the tray.

Much to Charlotte's surprise, the morgue did not smell like dead bodies. In fact, it smelled like the rest of the hospital. She looked over to the right and saw a leaky faucet. *Where did it go?* She wondered.

When Charlotte looked to her left again, she noticed that one of the tools was missing. She started breathing heavily. The corpse was behind her head, holding the scalpel at a 90-degree angle, ready to dig in. Piercing screams echoed throughout the small room, "Help!" She cried.

The light in the room dimmed a bit as the corpse carved a crooked line under her jugular with the scalpel. Its face curved into a sneer at the sound of Charlotte's screams.

The sound of Charlotte's heart flat-lining sent nurses rushing around trying to shock her heart. It was no use though and they knew that, yet they kept trying anyway.

One of the nurses had to leave the room at the sight of a teenager dying alone in a hospital bed. They concluded that she'd died in her sleep, something that wasn't too unusual for diabetics.

The corpse of the small girl was all that was left in the hospital bed. The white blanket was bundled around her feet. Her brown hair was sprawled out and shaped like the rays of the sun, contrasting with the bright white pillow underneath her head.

ABOUT THE AUTHOR

Maya Scianna

Maya is a freelance writer who enjoys writing fiction and invoking emotions within readers.

She mostly ghostwrites content for websites but will jump on the opportunity to write fiction stories, especially thrillers.

She currently has a website where she keeps a portfolio of stories she's written and a blog where she shares tips and her writing process.

When she's not writing, she's either reading, binging TV shows on Netflix, playing video games on her Switch, or looking for a new place to travel to.

You can reach Maya through her website: www.mscreative.online

Alternatively, her email is mayabree@gmail.com

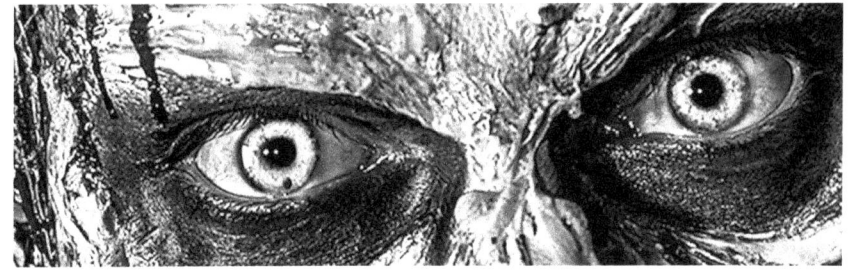

"MY DAD DID"

By Chase Wilkinson

"My Dad Did". We couldn't figure out what it meant. On the night of the murder, Sally wrote those three words. She was only two years old.

Now that we know, we wish she'd been able to tell us what had happened with her words, except Sally was a slow developer. She was a late walker, a late talker, and a late bloomer. Not just that, but she was born with a terrible stutter that impeded her speech.

For the first few years since her birth, she never spoke. She would only ever write down what she was thinking, and most of the time, there would be punctuation missing or spelling errors, so no one could ever make out what she was writing.

Our family cat, Whiskers, died mysteriously about a year after Sally was born. That poor cat endured a lot. We often found Sally pulling at its tail until it shrieked, clapping her hands and giggling with delight at Whisker's cries of agony.

Weirdly enough, Whiskers never scratched her. He hissed at her whenever she came crawling towards him, but despite the torment she put him through, Sally was always unharmed.

Our mother dismissed it as "simple curiosity at such a young age" and that was that. She never punished Sally. Come to think of it, she was probably scared of her.

Sally was born with a deformity. We found out that it was called "Anencephaly" – a serious birth defect where part of the brain or skull is missing. As a result, she suffered from what the lab coats called "stunted growth" as an infant.

She was also born blind, deaf, unconscious, and unable to feel pain.

Normally, anencephaly would kill a baby within the first few years of its life. We did some research and discovered that babies born with anencephaly hardly ever survive the birthing process; the longest recorded survivor only lasted until 28 months without life-sustaining interventions. Against all odds and all scientific logic, Sally survived the defect.

From that point onwards, we knew that she was special. Not the kind of special that would become a successful lawyer and live in a mansion, or open an art gallery and be a Picasso copycat.

Sally was another kind of special – the scary kind. In the same way that we fear the supernatural, we feared whatever allowed that baby to live through the impossible.

At 8 months old, Sally said her first word. It wasn't "mama" or "dadda" or even "sis". Sally said "Ke" and then "ko".

She had a limited range of speech, so she would split her words in half to make them more manageable. Mother kneeled down and said "Keko? Who's that?", but Sally just stared.

She wasn't staring *at* her, she was staring *through* her. Mother said that she felt like someone was standing behind her, but she and Sally were the only ones in the room.

Ever since, when Sally said "Keko", our mother would discourage it. She would say "mama" and "dadda" and "sis", but Sally would only ever say Keko.

Children have an active imagination. Everyone knows that. Sally would clap her hands and giggle and gurgle nonsense when she sat on the couch. This was when she had learned to sit up by herself (with supervision) and could watch TV or see the neighbors walking their dogs.

We all watched her as she had what we could only assume was a full-blown conversation with whomever she was talking to. That was just a guess, since it was all baby spit and gibberish to us.

As this behavior persisted, we soon learned to accept that Sally had an imaginary friend. At least, that was what we pretended it was.

Her imaginary friend was called "Keko". That brings us to Sally's second word, or should we say, "words" – plural. She said, "dem" "mom", which delighted our mother, since "mom" was an educated step toward addressing her as a parental figure.

Still, we put those words together and "demmom" made no sense at all. We were less thrilled when Sally only used the word once. We never heard it again.

It was only when she turned two that Sally finally got to grips with "dadda" and "mamma". We still couldn't get her to say "sis", but honestly, that was expected. When we were told that Sally's speech would remain broken for at least a few more years, our parents devised the idea of teaching Sally to write.

They did this over a course of months, painstakingly helping her hold the pencil and learn the alphabet and its shapes. Before long, she had mastered the art of writing. Not quite the Picasso we wanted, but close enough.

She wrote, "DAD" and "MOM" and even "SIS", which we were all thrilled about. Unsurprisingly, she wrote "KEKO" more than anything else.

Even though she could write, longer sentences would always contain punctuation or spelling errors and wouldn't always make sense.

We discovered that Sally would write the words that she heard most often, which proved to be an issue, since my parent's most-used words were either curse words or insults. They argued relentlessly. On-and-off most days. Our neighbors would relay backyard chit-chat over the fence like "why are they still together" and "they should get divorced".

They know about Sally; she was precisely the "unholy" baby that they blamed the relationship breakdown on. Sally would pester the neighbors' pets and leave their kids with bumps and bruises.

It was ridiculous for grown adults to blame such senseless violence on a newborn, but at some point, the complaints started to file in so frequently that it became harder to dismiss than it did to believe.

Sally had proven that she was capable of inflicting pain, just like she did with Whiskers, but an infant could never injure a child that was double her size. That was the excuse that our parents came up with to fend off the hounding neighbors.

After her second birthday, we noticed that the incidents with Sally got worse. It started to get uncontrollable. She misbehaved at every opportunity and when asked *why* she had drawn graphic images on the walls and broken her toys, her response was always "Keko".

Mother would be furious, cursing the day that Sally was even born, but whenever something went wrong, Sally would just point to an empty spot and say "Keko".

We had a fishbowl in our lounge – stored on the highest shelf. That way, it was completely out of reach. One evening, when our father came home from work, the fishbowl had been tipped over. All of the fish were scattered along the carpet, some of them still twitching as they suffocated.

All hell broke loose. My father demanded answers and when Sally got the blame, he hit me. For whatever reason, Sally started screaming. Not crying, just screaming.

Her scream reached such a high decibel that it almost shattered the windows. My father and I covered our ears, recoiled, and fled. When mother came home, she was horrified to learn about the tragic news regarding the dead fish, but even more infuriated to know that my father had assaulted me.

Another argument ensued, and a furious exchange led to the phrases "I wish I'd never met you" and "I want a divorce" being tossed around from both sides. Ultimately, our nosy neighbors intervened and phoned the police.

Since there was evidence of physical assault from the bruise on my cheekbone, my father was escorted out of the property. To this, my mother rejoiced and told him to "never to come back". Secretly, she must have been waiting for that moment for a very long time.

Weeks passed and Sally's mysterious mood swings seemed to calm somewhat. Perhaps our father had been a negative influence on all of us.

She still relied on "Keko" to keep herself entertained, but her mother was just glad to be rid of her beastly husband. He kept calling, pestering her, trying to change her mind with apologies and empty promises. Mother knew that silver-tongue all too well, so they cut contact after that.

Around a week later, his car appears outside our house. Mother threatens to call the police, but he insists that all he wants to do is talk. She humors him, letting him inside for short spell.

During that time, they discuss an effective plan moving forward. He never gave me an apology for hitting me, but I'd come to expect just as much. He never apologized for a lot of things, least of all his temper.

When tensions rise and the conversation gets heated, Sally starts to bawl. It was almost as if the shouting displeased her. She wept and thrust her tiny fists against the couch cushions as she did, chanting "Keko" desperately.

Suddenly, the lights went out. When we looked outside, the neighbors were unaffected. It was just our house. We all thought that to be unusual, since a power outage would affect the entire grid of connecting houses and not just ours.

Regardless, mother and father quieted down, as did Sally, but only briefly. Hateful words ended their relationship once and for all and our father cursed both me and my sister, essentially denouncing himself as our parent. Needless to say, there were no tears shed for him.

He stormed out, all outraged and heartbroken. That was the last time any of us saw him alive. After that, it was peaceful for a few days.

Mother struggled to sustain us by herself. Her wage barely covered the grocery bill, much less the household bills. We were poor, but at least my father was out of the picture. Little did we know, it would be a permanent departure.

One evening, just after a disappointing dinner, we all settled down to watch the six o'clock news. Sally was sat comfortably on her mother's lap, writing just like she always did.

Mother and I stared intently at the screen, learning all about the economical downfall and the latest invention that would "revolutionize technology as we know it".

Sally tittered happily, scrawling on the paper with a cheerful disposition that was so misplaced that it felt suspicious. Mother leaned over her shoulder, reading the phrase that Sally had written: "My Dad Did".

She looked puzzled, whispering in Sally's ear, "What did Daddy do?" By now, she had managed to say "Daddy" without wanting to vomit, but still refused to name him.

The news played its signature jingle, introducing the six o'clock highlights. When the top story was announced, we heard my father's name. It chilled my mother to the bone.

Her face turned pale, like she'd seen a ghost. "Local man dies in an apparent suicide." Father had stabbed himself with a kitchen knife. The landlord expressed his concerns when the apartment seemed vacated for a few days.

When the ambulance arrived on the scene, they stated that he had been dead for at least 24 hours. Paramedics commented that no one would have known he was there if not for the neighbor calling on a hunch.

Sally broke the silence by shrieking "Keko" and waving at the nothingness in the corner of the room. Mother exchanged glances with me, and then she carefully took the scrap paper out of Sally's tiny hands, despite her immediate protest. Knowing what she knew, she read the phrase again, just one 'e' short. *My Dad Did.*

ABOUT THE AUTHOR
Chase Wilkinson

For over 7 years, Chase has been a noteworthy presence within creative media. As a self-proclaimed geek and driven by a passion for horror, comic books, video games, and modern cinema, she takes pride in providing only the best publications.

She likes to label herself as an innovative writer doing what she loves, especially when it concerns her favorite interests. Aside from personal written projects, she can be credited as an award-winning screenwriter, published poet, and accomplished academic writer.

They have taken the media industry by storm, producing short stories, screenplays, articles, features, and poetry that thoroughly engage, excite and thrill those fortunate enough to read them. They enjoy watching anime, horror movies, and animated shows; their life revolves around cinema, video games, and

Chase can be reached on: Instagram @chaseswilkinson.

Alternatively, they can be contacted via email: chasesidney32@gmail.com

CHECK OUT THESE TITLES

Creepy Nightmares

Scary Short Stories For Teens Book 1, 2 & 3

MORE CREEPY BOOKS
COMING SOON!

ND STORIES TO TELL IN THE DARK: BOOK 1

www.ingramcontent.com/pod-product-compliance
Ingram Content Group UK Ltd.
Pitfield, Milton Keynes, MK11 3LW, UK
UKHW022241230426
12048UKWH00018BA/1388